The Moonies

JOURNEY TO THE TOTAL SOLAR ECLIPSE

Written by
MEG JERIT

Illustrated by
TAMAR BLAAUW

Published by American Paper Optics, LLC
www.eclipseglasses.com

First published in 2022
Directed by Jason Lewin
Written by Meg Jerit
Illustrated by Tamar Blaauw
Book design by Bryony van der Merwe
Character Design by William Chiles

ISBN: 979-8-218-10272-2

DEDICATION

For all the **AMAZING PARENTS** in our universe who support, inspire, and **ENCOURAGE ADVENTURE.**

The sky deepens into lavender over the sleeping planet of **MARS,** where the **MOONIE** family members slumber peacefully...

ALL EXCEPT ONE.

PROFESSOR LOONEY MOONIE hadn't been able to sleep all week. All night long, his big brown eyes had been glued to the eyepiece of the giant telescope emerging from their roof.

"Honey! You've got to see this - **COME LOOK!**"

Professor Moonie waved her to come near.

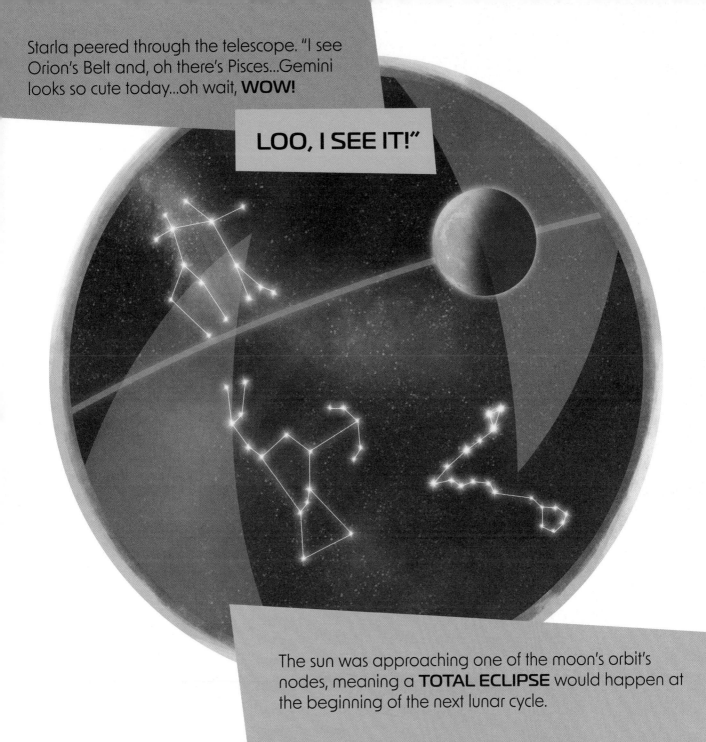

Starla peered through the telescope. "I see Orion's Belt and, oh there's Pisces...Gemini looks so cute today...oh wait, **WOW!**

LOO, I SEE IT!"

The sun was approaching one of the moon's orbit's nodes, meaning a **TOTAL ECLIPSE** would happen at the beginning of the next lunar cycle.

"The kids are going to be **PSYCHED!**"
Professor Moonie smiled.

Starla nodded but folded her lips; she had a **FEELING** the kids would not be psyched.

Last time the Moonies tried to catch an eclipse, it was a **DISASTER.**

They traveled through **TWO DIMENSIONS** only to discover they had been looking at the wrong moon the whole time, and then had a long, bumpy journey back through a black hole.

But Professor Moonie was already on his way to **TELL THE KIDS.**

Sunny and Crater were in the kitchen eating **STARFLAKES.** The family dog, Shadow, was waiting beneath the table for a stray marshmallow to fall.

"Wait so, what's going on?" Sunny was blinking rapidly; she had been sending **TELEPATHIC MESSAGES** to her boyfriend, Jupiter.

"Dad said we're going **ECLIPSE HUNTING** again" Crater sighed, tousling Shadow's ears. Sunny closed her eyes and went back to sending messages.

"Aw come on, Sunny Bunny! It'll be fun! Right, Crater?" Professor Moonie poured some **STARDUST** into his coffee.

"FOR SURE..." Crater agreed without looking at his dad. At age eleven, he'd rather be playing astro-ball with his friends than space traveling.

Starla sat down at the table with her children and winked at them. "It'll be different this time, and we've got another cycle of the **MOON** before we go."

Sunny raised her eyebrows; Crater offered a small smile.

"It's going to be so **HARD TO BE PATIENT!**" Professor Moonie bounced over, unaware of the rolling eyes.

All the Moonies were in the **ROCKET** and Mars was fading fast behind them. Sunny was blinking back tears because this was the weekend of Galaxy High's prom, and Crater was fighting motion sickness.

"Okay kids, now that we're out of the **ATMOSPHERE**, let's see what we know!"

Starla booed quietly, trying to get the kids to laugh. Crater perked up at the potential distraction.

"Starla, my love, **WHERE ARE WE HEADED** and why?" Professor Moonie said.

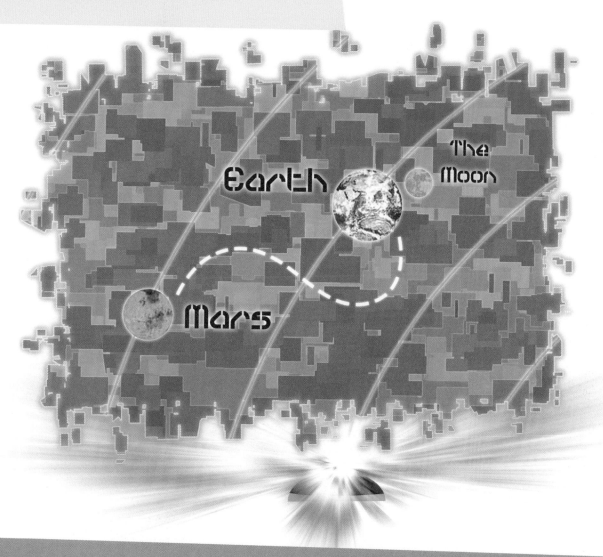

"Oh, I'm so glad you asked, Loo! This ship is headed straight for the state of **TEXAS, U.S.A.** where we will witness an eclipse from an earthly point of view..." Starla smiled at the kids in the back.

"Crater, what makes this **ECLIPSE** extra special for us to witness?" Professor Moonie couldn't help the excitement in his voice, and it was becoming contagious.

"Well, Dad, It's a **TOTAL ECLIPSE**. So, based on where we are located at that instant, we may perceive a total darkness befall the land!" Crater announced playfully into his sister's direction.

Starla clapped and Professor Moonie giggled, **"WHY YES!"**

Crater continued, "And also, I do know that if you **COMPARE SIZES,** the earth could be like the size of a pea, the sun would be an extra-large pizza, and the moon would be as little as a peppercorn."

"Wow, Crater! You're right on track! Now, who can tell me about the **UMBRA?"** Professor Moonie knew his daughter loved that word.

The Sun

← The Moon

The Earth →

Sunny smirked out the window before sighing. "During a total eclipse, the umbra is the **TOTAL SHADOW CAST** when the moon passes in front of the sun, which means the moon appears larger to us than the sun, if standing on earth."

Professor Moonie held his wife's hand and whistled. "This is going to be **OUT OF THIS WORLD!** I know last time was a letdown, but I have a good feeling about this one."

Starla cranked up the music, and the Moonies enjoyed
the **MILKY WAY HIGHWAY** from Mars to Austin, Texas.

"**OH, MY STARS!**" Starla said when they stepped off the rocket, "Are we on the Sun!?"

Shadow started panting immediately. The land all around them was kissed in heat and bright colors. Professor Moonie passed out water and **SUNSCREEN** to his family.

"**TEXANS ARE TOUGH,** I guess. This heat is next level. Where'd Crater and Shadow go? Shadow?"

The Moonies swiveled their heads around until they spotted a little boy and a dog devouring tacos at a picnic table by a **TACO TRUCK.**

"Check out this **SALSA!** This is a whole different galaxy of flavor!"

TACOS

SALSA

Everyone laughed and sat down together at the **PICNIC TABLE.**

"Okay, t-minus forty-five Earth minutes until show time. It's time for the retelling of the **ECLIPSE MYTHOLOGIES** over the centuries.

LOONEY, you want to start us off?" Starla asked as the family, now full, settled into their blanket on the grass.

"Sure thing, star-cakes. Well, in this very land, the **NATIVE PEOPLES** of the Americas believed a total eclipse of the sun to be a threat, and they would shoot **FLAMING ARROWS** toward the Sun in an attempt to re-ignite it!"

Starla nodded and added, "And in **CHINA,** the eclipse was believed to be caused by a dragon eating the sun. To frighten the dragon away, people would **PLAY DRUMS,** remember? Sunny, what happened in 585 B.C.?"

Sunny was telepathically texting, and Crater elbowed her. "Hey! Oh, there was an eclipse during a **WAR** in **TURKEY,** and the two armies took that to be a sign to lay down their weapons."

Starla grinned and squeezed her daughter's hand. Shadow whined.

"What, Shadow? Oh!" Starla looked up to see **GIANT STORM CLOUDS** gathering right over downtown Austin, where the eclipse was about to take place.

Everyone looked at Professor Moonie, who was looking at Shadow. They could not miss this again.

"SHADOW! What do we do? Where do we go?"

Shadow panted and started chasing his tail, before suddenly stopping, his tail straight up and his nose pointed toward the **STATE CAPITOL**.

Crater looked deeply into the dog's eyes.

"Dad, come on we can't have come all the way down here only to **MISS IT**."

There were some **TEXAS HUMANS** (Texans) ambling around, chatting without looking up. They didn't even know they were about to miss a total solar eclipse!

SUDDENLY, Shadow bolted, and within moments was already a few yards away, his nose to the ground and his tail in the air.

"DAD! LOOK! COME ON!"

Crater called behind him as the Moonie family lined up in pursuit of their silvery shepherd who was headed straight for the **TEXAS STATE CAPITOL.**

Shadow was howling at the moving moon as the family chased him. He could smell the moon's **INCOMING SHADOW.** He knew in his doggy heart he had to get up to the top of the dome.

"HEY! What are these things?" Crater asked as the family dodged through a garden of cacti.

"DON'T TOUCH THEM!!" Professor Moonie called as he hurdled over three of them.

Shadow couldn't feel his legs anymore, and soon he was **LIFTING OFF** the ground. As he did, he noticed that the Moonies needed a way up to where he was.

He began to poop small **ASTEROIDS** that floated after him for the Moonies to step on. The astral rocks bobbed, unbothered by gravity.

"THANKS, SHADOW!" Crater called and each Moonie stepped up the asteroid ladder to the top of the Texas State Capitol.

Everyone reached the top and started hugging, but they couldn't **CELEBRATE** for long: they were only moments away from a total eclipse!

Professor Moonie passed out the solar eclipse glasses for safely viewing the **PARTIAL PHASES** of the eclipse just before totality. Sunny was smiling cheek to cheek as Starla held hands with Looney.

Crater cradled Shadow's head in his arms. They knew they were about to witness the most **AMAZING SIGHT** they had ever seen in all the galaxy.

Crickets began to chirp as the light dipped into itself. Then the moon **PERFECTLY ALIGNED** with the Sun.

The Moonies removed their **ECLIPSE GLASSES** to see totality with a perfect ring of light radiating from the beaming circle of night sky where the sun's familiar face had been.

The Moonies' bodies began to **GLOW** as if the moon was right underneath their skin.

"**DIVINE...**" Starla whispered.

"Photographs could never do this **JUSTICE,**" Sunny whispered back. Professor Moonie was crying.

When totality was over and the moon allowed the sun to shine again, everything began to return to normal except for the Moonies and all the people who had witnessed this **PHENOMENON.**

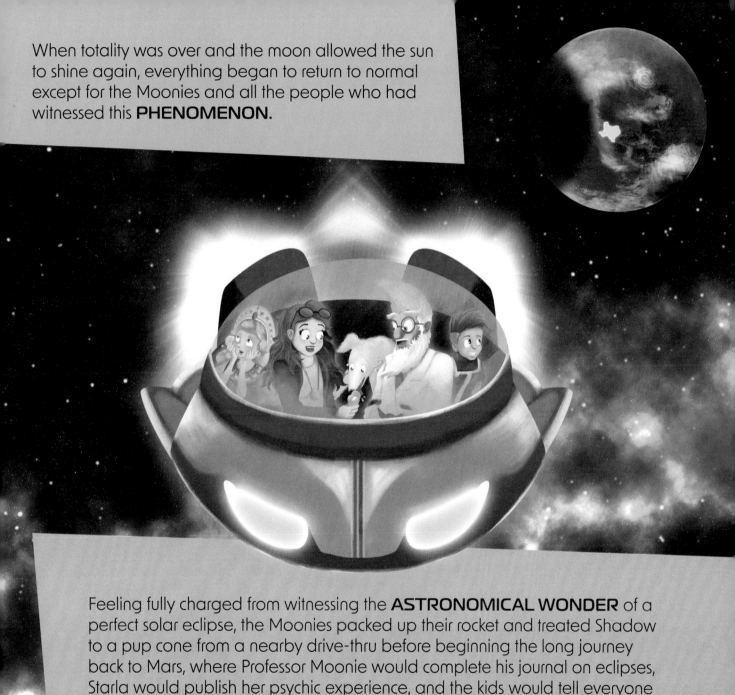

Feeling fully charged from witnessing the **ASTRONOMICAL WONDER** of a perfect solar eclipse, the Moonies packed up their rocket and treated Shadow to a pup cone from a nearby drive-thru before beginning the long journey back to Mars, where Professor Moonie would complete his journal on eclipses, Starla would publish her psychic experience, and the kids would tell everyone they knew the story of Shadow's asteroids saving this **MAGICAL DAY.**

ABOUT THE AUTHOR

Meg Jerit is a writer, editor, and creative healer. She is earning her Bachelor of Arts in English from Rhodes College, and her MFA in creative nonfiction from Columbia College Chicago.

Her poetry and prose can be found in various journals, and she has attended The Kenyon Review Writers Workshop.

She currently lives in Austin, Texas, with her partner and two shepherds, all of whom cannot wait to witness the magic and mystery of the total solar eclipse!